TRANSFORMERS
ROBOTS IN DISGUISE

Drift's Samurai Showdown

by John Sazaklis & Steve Foxe

LITTLE, BROWN AND COMPANY

New York   Boston

Little, Brown and Company

Hachette Book Group
1290 Avenue of the Americas, New York, NY 10104
Visit us at lb-kids.com

Little, Brown and Company is a division of Hachette Book Group, Inc.
The Little, Brown name and logo are trademarks of
Hachette Book Group, Inc.

The publisher is not responsible for websites (or their content)
that are not owned by the publisher.

First Edition: September 2015

ISBN 978-0-316-30192-3

10 9 8 7 6 5 4 3 2 1

RRD-C

Printed in the United States of America

Licensed By:

Sideswipe

Strongarm

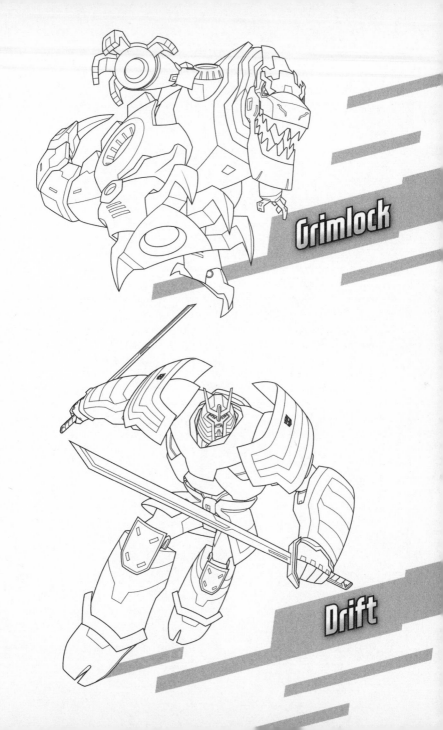

Grimlock

Drift

Chapter 1

"Decepticon attack!" Bumblebee shouts at his team. "The scrapyard has been breached!" He zooms through their makeshift Earth headquarters with his high-beam lights flashing and his horn blaring. "All bots to their stations! This is *not* a drill!"

1

Strongarm is the first Autobot to respond to Bee's alerts, switching straight from sleep mode to her robot form. This eager cadet is always at the ready.

"I'll protect the humans, sir!" she says, sprinting toward the vintage diner that Denny and Russell Clay call home. "I can see Sideswipe isn't up to the task!"

"Hey, this bot's always got his motor revving," replies Sideswipe, flexing his gears and

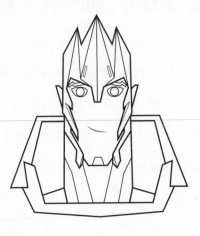

shaking out his sprockets. "It just so happens to be the middle of a night cycle, and I was getting my beauty recharge."

The flashy, young Sideswipe flips through the air and lands back-to-back against the straightlaced Strongarm.

Suddenly, the ground beneath them starts to rumble at the approach of pounding footsteps. The two Autobots draw their weapons.

"AWW YEAH, LET ME AT 'EM!" Grimlock roars, stomping his way toward the scrapyard's front gate.

The massive Dinobot is *always* itching to turn some Decepticons into scrap metal!

Bumblebee screeches to a halt in Grimlock's path, blocking his stampede.

"That's not the plan, Grim. Follow our breach protocol!"

Bumblebee spins his wheels while the Dino-bot complies and turns around. Grimlock joins his teammates at the diner, grumbling all the way.

Denny Clay stumbles out into the scrapyard he owns and operates, rubbing the sleep from his eyes and tying the belt on his vintage rockabilly flamingo robe a little tighter.

"What's all this racket? It's after midnight, you know," Denny pleads, stifling a yawn. "Humans actually *need* to sleep, remember?"

Bumblebee pulls up next to the diner and shifts into bot mode. With his lights still shining, the Autobot leader peers into the darkness of the scrapyard. There are no

Decepticons in sight. There's also no sign of Drift, the stoic and mysterious former bounty hunter who recently joined up with them.

"Where's Drift?" Bumblebee asks. "This breach-defense drill needs full cooperation to work."

Strongarm and Sideswipe exchange looks as they slowly realize the "Decepticon attack"

may not be as real as they had thought. They return their weapons to their holsters.

"Um, sir, did you say 'drill'?" Strongarm asks tentatively.

If any bot understands the need for preparedness, it's Strongarm, but that doesn't mean she appreciates being left in the dark by her commanding officer.

Russell Clay, Denny's twelve-year-old son, steps out from behind a row of antique washing machines. He clicks a stopwatch in his hand.

"Three minutes and forty-five seconds, Bee," Russell says. "Two minutes longer than your goal time."

"Scrap, that's no good. And Drift didn't even show up! I don't know about that bot...." Bumblebee sighs. "In the case of a Decepticon attack on the scrapyard during typical Earth rest hours, we should all be able to meet at Central Diner Defense Point Delta in under two minutes."

Grimlock is still ready to rumble. He looks around and slowly—more slowly than the other bots—realizes what's going on.

"Wait a nanocycle...you mean I don't get to demolish any Decepticons tonight?"

"No, Grim," Bumblebee explains. "This was meant to be a team-training exercise, but not all your teammates thought it was worth their time."

As the Autobots begin to disperse, Drift calmly joins the gathering, flanked by his two Mini-Cons, Jetstorm and Slipstream.

"Nice of you to show up," Sideswipe mumbles.

"It is wise of you to train your team, Bumblebee," Drift says dryly. "It is clear that they struggle with basic functions."

Drift's deadpan insult noticeably upsets Strongarm, who prides herself on her professionalism and combat readiness. "But I do not need training. I have survived on my own for many cycles," he continues.

Jetstorm coughs as if to remind Drift that he has been alone *except* for his Mini-Cons. Slipstream steps on Jetstorm's foot and quiets the less reserved of the two apprentice-bots. Drift is a stern master and doesn't appreciate his students speaking out of turn.

"I know you're used to working alone, Drift," Bumblebee says, taking on an air of authority. "And I'm happy to have you as part of our team here on Earth. But I won't stand for you insulti—"

BREEP! BREEP!

An alarm screeches over the speaker system installed on the diner's exterior.

"Decepticon attack! Please retort…resort… report to the command center at once!" The jumble of words is the telltale malfunction of Fixit, the Autobots' Mini-Con helper.

Denny Clay covers his ears with his hands.

"Is this another drill, Bee?" Denny yells over the siren. "If so, it's way past Rusty's bedtime—and mine!"

"If this is a drill, it's not one I planned!" Bumblebee yells back. "We better join Fixit and find out what's going on!"

Chapter 2

Once everyone gathers in the command
center, Fixit taps furiously at his console to
pull up a large hologram of the Decepticon
his systems discovered. The villainous bot is
short and round, with a masklike marking
over his eyes and a large tail circled by rings
of alternating black and brown metal.

"Aw yeah, I get to smash up a Decepticon!" Grimlock says, pounding his fists together.

"Hey, he looks like a raccoon!" Russell observes.

"What's a 'raccoon'?" Grimlock asks. "That's not like a"— he gulps —"kitten, is it?"

The typically bombastic Dinobot looks oddly nervous. He's not very good at hiding his bizarre fear of Earth felines.

"Actually, they're not closely related,"

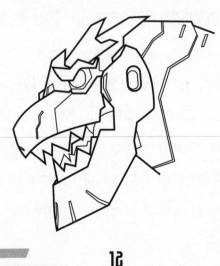

Russell says, easing Grimlock's mind slightly. "But they do look and act a little similar, I guess."

Grimlock suppresses a startled yelp.

"My sensors picked up a Decepticon moving through the side streets of Crown City," Fixit explains. "It appears that he is trying to stay hidden from humans, but who knows how long that will last!"

"All right, bots, we need to apprehend this Decepticon before he's spotted," Bee says, stepping up to lead his team.

"Oh, he's not spotted," Sideswipe remarks, pointing at the image. "He's striped, see?"

Bumblebee narrows his optics.

"What?" Sideswipe shrugs. "I may be

half-charged, but my funny bolt is always at one hundred percent!"

Ignoring the hotshot Autobot, Bumblebee continues with the task at hand.

"Grim, you'll have to stay behind. We'll be in the middle of the city, and you don't have a vehicle mode," he says.

The Dinobot tries to hide his relief.

"Fixit, what can you tell us about this criminal before we put wheels down and go to town?" Bumblebee asks.

Sideswipe groans over Bee's attempt at a catchphrase.

"Decepticon identification: Forager. Mercenary, bounty hunter, and rabble-rouser," Fixit says as he punches at the console processing data. "Arrested alongside other Decepticons calling themselves the Ronin."

Drift scoffs. "This Decepticon is not worth my time. I will provide you with my students, Jetstorm and Sliptstream, to assist in my absence."

Before Bumblebee can protest, Drift turns and walks out of the room.

"I guess someone never learned teamwork in lob-ball youth league," Sideswipe whispers loudly to Rusty.

"Okay, team, we don't have time for this. We've got to put wheels down and—"

"Bee!" the rest of the room shouts in unison, cutting off their leader's mediocre new rallying cry.

"Fine, let's just go capture this Decepticon," Bumblebee says, leaping into vehicle mode and leading his team out of the scrapyard.

Slipstream and Jetstorm jump onto Sideswipe's trailer and Strongarm brings up the rear. Grimlock and Fixit stay behind as the yawning pair of Clays shuffle off to bed.

The Autobots cut through the forest, cross

the bridge, and arrive in Crown City in no time. Using Fixit's coordinates, they quickly spot Forager in a dark alley behind an auto repair store.

The dexterous Decepticon is sifting through spare parts.

Bumblebee quietly directs Sideswipe to

take to the rooftops. The younger bot zooms out of view, switches back to bot mode, and leaps into the air with Slipstream and Jetstorm in tow.

Strongarm, in her police SUV mode, pulls around to block Forager's exit.

Once the whole team is in place, Bee honks his horn—*BEEP BEEP*—startling the Decepticon!

"Oh, scrud, guess I gotta bust up some natives!" Forager growls, tearing an old tire in two with his bare paws. "Let's dance!"

"Heads up!" Sideswipe yells, drawing his swords and dropping down from above.

The two Mini-Cons follow close behind.

Sideswipe slashes and slices his blades at Forager.

SWISH!

CLANG!

The Decepticon deflects the blows with his claws as showers of sparks light up the night sky.

Slipstream and Jetstorm lunge at Forager's legs.

The cranky crook hops from one foot to the other, trying to kick the Mini-Cons off.

"Looks like we are dancing after all!" says Jetstorm.

While Forager attempts to hold off his three ninja-like assailants, Strongarm and Bumblebee rev their engines and charge at the Decepticon.

In a flash, the two Autobots crunch Forager between their fenders!

SMASH!

The craven convict is down for the count.

"Good work, team," Bumblebee says.

The Autobots load Forager's unconscious frame onto the trailer, tie him down, and cover him with a tarp.

Bumblebee radios Fixit and asks the Mini-Con to prepare a stasis pod.

A short victory lap later, the bots arrive back at the scrapyard with their defeated target.

"My, that was fast!" Fixit exclaims, greeting the bots near the stasis pods. "Not much fight in this one?"

"This is just what happens when you work together, Fixit," Bumblebee says, scanning the scrapyard for Drift. "Too bad not everyone on this team seems to have gotten the memo."

As if on cue, Drift rounds the corner.

Slipstream and Jetstorm bow to their master.

"I am glad the mission went well," Drift says. "I trust my students were of sufficient help?"

Slipstream bows and pulls back the tarp to reveal a still-unconscious Forager. Drift gives a barely perceptible nod of approval.

Once the Mini-Con replaces the cover, Forager opens his optics. The raccoon-like bot was playing possum! He flexes his dexterous paws and two lockpicks pop out from the tips of his claws. With a swift twist of his wrist, Forager frees himself and makes a break for it, tossing the tarp at Drift and the Mini-Cons to distract them!

"So long, losers—"

WHAM!

Forager runs smack-dab into Grimlock.

"Looks like I got to demolish a Decepticon after all!" Grim says, proudly holding Forager down with one massive foot.

Bumblebee helps Grim load the struggling captive into the designated stasis pod.

"Let go of me! I have rights, you know!"

Forager yells, straining against Grimlock's powerful grip. "You can't lock me up just 'cause I'm a convicted criminal!"

Before the pod's cover slides shut, Forager gets a good look at the other bots. His optics lock on Drift.

"Hey! I know you!" Forager hollers, pointing at Drift through the stasis pod window. "From that Ronin job on the moon of Athena! You gotta get me outta here, pal!"

Before Forager can say anything else, Fixit finishes the stasis sequence and puts the dangerous Decepticon on ice.

Bumblebee quietly mouths Forager's words to himself, processing what was just said. He turns toward Drift.

"What did he mean by 'pal'?"

Drift tenses his shoulders. The mysterious samurai rests one hand on the hilt of his sword.

"My past is my own, Bumblebee. Do not assume you have any right to know about it."

Strongarm and Sideswipe move closer to Bumblebee's side.

"If you're going to work alongside my team, I think I have every right."

Jetstorm and Slipstream cast worried glances at their master, who refuses to meet their optics.

"If that is your stance, perhaps it is time I leave this team, Bumblebee." Drift quickly shifts into his vehicle mode and speeds out of the scrapyard!

As the dust settles, everyone exchanges grave looks.

Everyone except for Grimlock.

"So, uh, what just happened?"

Chapter 3

Denny Clay's alarm clock goes off at seven
o'clock the next morning. Crawling out of
bed to the sound of golden oldies, Denny's
first thought is that the Autobots can keep
their Energon—he just wants his coffee!

The Clays enjoy having Bee and the others around, but it can make for a lot of sleepless nights, something that exhausts Denny a bit more than it does his preteen son, Russell.

As the man shuffles outside half-awake, he stumbles upon a full-on Autobot interrogation, like something out of one of his favorite vintage cops versus gangsters films.

Slipstream and Jetstorm are sitting side-by-side on an overturned refrigerator. Bumblebee leans over the tiny bots, scowling, while Grimlock, Strongarm, and Sideswipe stand menacingly behind him.

"Youse better fess up or it's no more Mr. Nice-Bot!" Bumblebee says, affecting a bizarre accent.

"Whoa, guys, what's going on here?" Denny asks, sprinting toward them as fast as his retro bunny slippers will carry him. "And what's with that corny gangster act, Bee?"

"Sometimes you leave the TV on at night and that stuff starts to sink in," Bumblebee replies. "Besides, we tried asking nicely, but these two won't say a word."

"Why are you questioning your own guys?"

Denny asks, surprised at Bumblebee's behavior. "And where's Drift? I don't think he'd like you going off on his students like this."

"That's exactly the problem, sir," Strongarm pipes in. "Our newest Decepticon prisoner seemed to recognize Drift as a former ally, but Drift sped away before we could get any explanation out of him. Now we're questioning his Mini-Cons to try to uncover if Drift is actually an embedded Decepticon agent!"

Bumblebee steps forward to apologize to the frightened Slipstream and Jetstorm. Being a leader isn't easy. Even Optimus occasionally made the wrong call.

"I'm sorry. We might have...overreacted," Bumblebee says. "We're happy to have Drift and the two of you on the team, and it's admirable that you want to protect him, but we really need to know what's going on."

Slipstream and Jetstorm look at each other, their optics widening and narrowing in wordless conversation. Jetstorm opens his mouth to speak, but Slipstream glares at him to stay quiet.

Soon, Russell Clay wanders outside, sleepy-eyed and confused.

"What's going on out here, Bee?" Russell asks.

After Bee fills Russell in on the Mini-Cons' strict silence, Russell steps forward to take charge.

"Why don't you let me have a shot with

them?" Russell asks, cracking his knuckles. Slipstream and Jetstorm would have been intimidated, but it's hard to be scared of an Earth boy in cartoon-print pajamas. "Give me a few minutes and I'll have them singing like stool pigeons."

"I don't need them to sing; I just need them to talk," Bumblebee says, prompting an exaggerated eye roll from Russell.

"I know I can do it," Russell says with confidence. "But you'd better give us some space. Except for you, Sideswipe. You should stay."

Everyone else reluctantly heads to the opposite end of the scrapyard. Denny shoots Russell a look of concern before he goes, but Russell gives his dad a thumbs-up. Once the others are out of sight, Russell climbs onto Sideswipe's shoulders.

"Okay, boys, it's time to play rough," he says, looming over the Mini-Cons. "Tag, you're it!"

Russell leans down and slaps Jetstorm on the shoulder, then shouts at Sideswipe to run. After a moment's confusion, Sideswipe grins and runs off through one of the winding corridors of junk and old trash that makes up the scrapyard.

Jetstorm and Slipstream share a puzzled glance before Jetstorm cracks a sly grin, too, and runs off after Sideswipe. With a drawn-out sigh, Slipstream follows.

"Tag, you're it!" Jetstorm shrieks, knocking Sideswipe on the knee.

"Not for long!" Sideswipe replies, leaping backward to bop an unamused Slipstream on the head. "Tag! Your turn!"

Slipstream grumbles and refuses to move, but he can't deny wanting to play, too. He runs after his fellow Mini-Con and tags him, keeping the game in motion until Russell is a sweaty mess and the three bots are running on fumes.

They all meet back by the diner and plop down near the overturned fridge.

"So, how does that count as interrogation, Russell Clay?" Jetstorm asks, stretching out his joints.

"It doesn't. I figured you get enough of that just by being Drift's students," Russell replies. "He's really tough on you two."

Slipstream and Jetstorm look at each other and slowly nod.

"Master Drift *is* tough on us, but it's for our own good," Slipstream says, defending their master. "And whatever he's doing now, whatever reason he has for leaving, must be a good one."

"So you don't know why that Decepticon might act like he knew Drift?" Russell asks.

"Master Drift shares lessons with us, not his life story," Slipstream replies.

Jetstorm coughs and nudges Slipstream in the side. Slipstream tries to act like he doesn't notice, but Jetstorm does it again—and again. Finally, Slipstream comes out with it.

"Okay, fine!" Slipstream whispers angrily. "Master Drift did tell us one thing that is probably important...."

Russell and Sideswipe lean in to hear Slipstream's hushed information.

"Before Master Drift was Master Drift," explains Slipstream, "he went by another name: Deadlock. And under that name, Master Drift wasn't the honorable Autobot hero you know today—he was a Decepticon!"

Chapter 4

"Drift used to be a Decepticon?! Are you serious?" Bumblebee shouts, leaping out from behind a pile of old bicycles. "We let a traitor into our ranks?"

Strongarm climbs out from her own hiding spot under a stack of vintage carousel horses.

"You couldn't have known, sir!" she says.

"Decepticons are deceptive—why, it's right there in the name! Although, there is protocol in place for background checks. If you had read handbook entry eight hundred sixteen, subsection eighty-seven, you'd know that...."

"Not helpful, Strongarm!" Russell says. "And were you guys spying on us? Didn't you trust us?!"

"Yeah, didn't you trust them, Bee?" Grimlock asks, peering down from the roof of a nearby retired school bus. Russell shoots him an accusing look. "Hey, don't look at me. I just come up here to catch some sun once in a while." The Dinobot lies back down on his perch and stretches out, excusing himself from the conversation.

Bumblebee stands up to address Russell and the Mini-Cons.

"I do trust you, Russell, and I appreciate the honesty, Slipstream and Jetstorm," he says. "But this is very serious. If Drift was communicating with Forager, he might also have been communicating with Steeljaw or other, even worse Decepticons. He could have been getting close to us to feed them intel on how to attack Earth."

"Master Drift would never betray his word!" Slipstream shouts. "Master Drift is a bot of honor. He would never betray...us."

Slipstream hangs his head in disappointment. Jetstorm moves to comfort his brother-in-arms, but Slipstream pulls away.

Sideswipe mulls over everything he's heard

from Slipstream and Bumblebee, along with the scene he witnessed last night. The typically hasty bot tries to recall exactly what Forager said to Drift before the stasis pod closed.

"Hey, Bee, I just thought of something," Sideswipe says. "Forager said he recognized Drift from a moon or something, but it wasn't an instant thing, right? He had to think about it first."

Slipstream and Jetstorm look up at Sideswipe hopefully.

"So maybe Drift does have, you know, a past—just like Grim—but it's all behind him now, and he's just ashamed to admit it? We've all done things we aren't proud of."

Bumblebee considers this thoughtfully.

Grimlock leans back over the roof of the bus to nod encouragingly.

"Well, sir, Sideswipe may be right," Strongarm says, "but we have to consider the possibility that Drift is no longer allied with Forager and is afraid of compromising plans with other Decepticons."

Slipstream and Jetstorm both groan in frustration.

"I'm sorry, sir, but we can't afford to take chances," Strongarm adds. "We've already witnessed infighting among the Decepticons, so we need to be prepared for any outcome."

"I'm afraid Strongarm is right," Bumblebee says, addressing the Mini-Cons. "It might be hard to hear, but we have to brace ourselves for the worst until we can find Drift and get his side of this. And it doesn't make me optimistic that he sped off when we tried to discuss it."

The Autobots and Russell slowly trudge back toward the diner, their minds swirling with thoughts of betrayal and mistrust.

Suddenly, Fixit's voice crackles over the speaker system.

"This is not a drill! Multiple Decepticon signals located!"

The Autobots all rush to the command

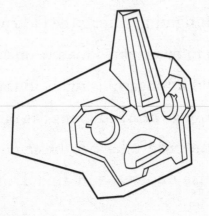

center, where Fixit pulls up a holographic map. Two red beacons flash in the quarry a few miles from the scrapyard.

"Fixit, can you pull up information on these new Decepticons so we know who we're facing?" Bee asks.

Fixit's digits click-clack across the keyboard. He buzzes with confusion.

"I'm afraid not, Bee," Fixit replies. "It looks like these Decepticons have obscured their signals!"

"Can you look up another signal for us?" Strongarm asks. "Can you track Drift?"

The Mini-Con goes back to speedily typing away. After a moment, Fixit shouts, "Aha!" and turns back around.

"Our systems are too weak to pick up most general bot signals unless they're in the immediate area, but by rerouting the signal booster through the Energon relay—"

"Cut to the chase, please, Fixit," Bumblebee interrupts politely.

"Base...case...I mean, 'chase' indeed, Bee!" Fixit replies, pointing to the screen. "There's a signal that matches Drift's size and shape moving right toward the two Decepticons!"

Slipstream and Jetstorm give each other worried looks—as do Bee and Strongarm, but for different reasons.

"We must find and assist Master Drift!" Jetstorm pleads. "We don't know how powerful those Decepticons might be, and he's headed right for them!"

Bumblebee agrees with the Mini-Con. He orders everyone to gather up and head out, except for Jetstorm and Slipstream. The disappointment is clear on their faces.

"You two stay behind and protect Russell, Denny, and Fixit in case one of the Decepticons breaks away and comes here," Bee instructs. "We'll go help your master."

The two smaller bots reluctantly accept the Autobot leader's commands. Bee changes into his shiny yellow vehicle mode and leads Strongarm, Sideswipe, and Grimlock out the gate, racing into the woods toward the three signals.

Once they're out of earshot of the others, Strongarm drives up close to Bee and whispers to her commanding officer.

"Sir, you know there's a possibility that Drift is moving toward the Decepticons *on purpose*, right?" Strongarm says. She hesitates, not wanting to finish saying what she's thinking. "That he might be meeting up with his—"

"Don't say it, Strongarm," Bee interrupts. "I know what you're thinking. And I'm afraid your suspicion might be right. Drift isn't accidentally heading toward trouble—he's meeting up with his Decepticon allies to cause it!"

Chapter 5

As Bumblebee, Strongarm, Sideswipe, and Grimlock race toward the Decepticon beacons, Russell does his best to keep Drift's anxious Mini-Cons occupied at the scrapyard.

"Tag, you're it!" Russell shouts, bopping Jetstorm on the shoulder and running off. The Mini-Con does not move to follow.

"I am not it, Russell Clay," Jetstorm replies morosely. "Unless 'it' means 'depressed.'"

Russell frowns. He turns to his dad for help.

"Hey, guys!" Denny says in his characteristically cheery voice. "I just got a shipment of retro video-game cartridges, and I need help blowing on them to see which ones still work. Think you guys are fit for duty?"

Jetstorm and Slipstream are too honor-bound to resist a call to help. They both stand at once and bow to Denny.

"We will assist you in your task, Denny Clay," they say in unison.

"Yeah, that sounds great!" Fixit adds. "Maybe while we do that, I can tell you all about how I once subdivided the power coupler to—"

"Sure thing, Fixit," Denny says, cutting him off. "Whatever floats your boat."

"Oh, Denny Clay," Fixit chuckles. "This was on a trans-galactic space shuttle, not a boat! Really, humans are so odd sometimes."

As the Clays keep the Mini-Cons occupied, the Autobots zoom through the woods toward the flashing beacons. Bee screeches to a stop at the edge of the forest where the trees clear and the land slopes down into the quarry.

"Okay, bots, this is where Fixit's tracker

leads," Bumblebee whispers, changing into robot mode and peering down at the device in his hands. "That means Drift should be right...there!"

Bumblebee points across the quarry, where Drift's sleek sports car form kicks up a storm of dust. "But where are the Decepticons? The tracker shows that Drift is nearly on top of them."

"Maybe they're camouflaged!" suggests Strongarm.

"Maybe they're really small!" offers Sideswipe.

"Maybe they're ghosts!" adds Grimlock, prompting blank looks from his teammates. "What? Rusty always makes me watch scary movies with him. You never know!"

Bumblebee quiets his team. As they watch, Drift rushes right past the Decepticon signals and plows into the forest on the other side of the quarry.

"There's something strange going on here," Bumblebee says, leaping into vehicle mode once more. "Follow me."

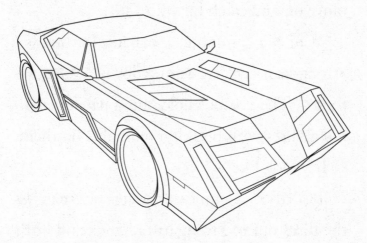

The Autobot leader steers down into the quarry, taking the same path Drift just blazed. The dust is still settling when they arrive at the location of the beacons. Bumblebee, Strongarm, and Sideswipe switch back to their bot modes.

"Great, so Fixit created another busted invention," Sideswipe says, looking around the seemingly empty quarry. "Can we get a move on and catch up with Drift?"

"Wait a minute, exhaust-for-brains," Strong-arm says, crouching down. "What are these?" The law-bot holds up a pair of small metal discs with blinking red lights on them. "They look like—"

"BOMBS!" Grimlock shouts. He snatches the discs out of Strongarm's hands and hurls them across the quarry. "EVERYONE, DOWN!" The Dinobot hits the ground with a thud and the other bots follow. After a minute with no explosion, Sideswipe raises his head.

"Uhh, guys, shouldn't we have blown up by now?" the young Autobot says, peering around.

"Be quiet, Sideswipe!" Strongarm hisses.

"Explosive ordinance protocol clearly states that—"

"Hold that thought, cadet," Bumblebee

says, springing up and running in the direction of the discs. Bumblebee picks one up, checks the tracker in his hand, and then hurls the disc back in the direction of the other Autobots, scattering them. "I knew it!"

Strongarm carefully peers out from behind a boulder. "Knew what, sir?"

"These aren't bombs. They're fake Decepticon signals," Bumblebee says, picking up the remaining disc and crushing it between his digits. "Someone left them here to distract us and get us away from the scrapyard." Bumblebee quickly dials Fixit on his communicator, but the quirky little Mini-Con doesn't pick up. "Forget Drift, we need to get back now!"

Unbeknownst to Team Bee, another set of bots is on their way toward the scrapyard. Just inside the tree line that surrounds the yard's outer fence, two escaped prisoners conspire and plot.

They are the dangerous Decepticons known as Foxtrot and Stilts. Foxtrot is a cunning and sly rust-colored bot, with a big round tail and pointed, alert audio sensors. Stilts is

all length: long legs, long neck, long beak—
with a gleaming white sheen and a bright red
crown that glints in the sun.

Both bots are safely under the cover of the
signal disruption field built into Stilts's large
wings.

"It looks like those disgusting do-gooder
Autobots just found my signal decoys," Foxtrot hisses, tapping at a console embedded in
his tail. "The microcameras captured two of
them. I'll program holo-cloaks of each, and
we can waltz into their compound with ease.
My scans show that there are just three Mini-
Cons left inside."

Foxtrot punches in a few more codes and
two small discs pop out of his tail. "Here,

you take the big green one, and I'll keep the nerdy-looking yellow one."

The Decepticons fix the discs to their chests, press a button, and, in a flash, they're covered in pitch-perfect holograms of Grimlock and Bumblebee!

"A Dinobot?" Stilts says, looking down at himself with a wicked laugh. "Guess I'll have to act extra dumb to match my new look."

Inside the diner, Fixit gets a ping that the perimeter sensors have been tripped. He pulls up a visual of "Grimlock" and "Bumblebee" walking toward the scrapyard's entrance, limping and looking wounded. Denny tells

Russell to stay put and tasks Jetstorm to watch him.

Denny, Fixit, and Slipstream sprint out to attend to the disguised Decepticons at the front gate.

"Bee, are you okay?" Denny asks. "What happened to Sideswipe and Strongarm?"

"And Master Drift!" Slipstream adds.

The bot they believe to be Grimlock cracks an awful smile full of sharp teeth. He unhooks a capsule from his waist and tosses it at Slipstream and Denny.

WHOOSH!

It explodes into a giant net on impact, trapping the two of them tightly inside!

"Nothing...yet," Stilts sneers.

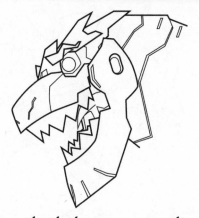

He drops the hologram, revealing himself as a tall birdlike Decepticon.

Fixit tries to zoom away, but pretend-Bumblebee snatches him up.

"Not so fast, scrap metal," Foxtrot says, dropping his hologram.

He dangles the Mini-Con upside down.

"You're going to show us where you're keeping Forager. The Ronin may not follow any masters, but we take care of our own!"

Chapter 6

"Did you hear something?" Russell asks, nervously peering out the diner windows. Jetstorm gently pulls the young human back.

"Let me take a look first, Russell Clay," Jetstorm says, steeling himself for action. "I am honor-bound to protect you under your master's orders."

Russell rolls his eyes. "He's not my master, Jetstorm. He's my dad!"

Jetstorm slinks silently out the diner door. He quickly freezes in his tracks when he sees Stilts approach with Denny and Slipstream strung over his shoulder in a net! Jetstorm darts inside and pulls Russell into a back room. The front door creaks slightly as it closes.

"What was that?" Stilts asks, bending his long crane-like neck toward the sound. "I thought there were only three Mini-Cons left on this base."

Denny twists around in the net.

"I, uh, dropped my hubcap," he says.

Stilts peers over his shoulder at his captives.

"You're an odd-looking bot," the Decepticon

observes. "A little…soft to be a Cybertronian."

"Beep boop bop?" Denny replies.

He wiggles in the bag, doing his best impression of a robotic dance that was popular in his youth. It is not very convincing.

Stilts glares and keeps walking.

Once they are gone, Jetstorm emerges from the back room and peeks outside again.

"Your master and my brother-in-arms have

been captured, Russell Clay!" Jetstorm whispers to Russell. "The ones we thought to be Bumblebee and Grimlock must have been… Decepticons in disguise! We must escape! Climb onto my back and hold tight."

With Russell clinging to him, Jetstorm slips out the diner's back door and begins hopping, ninja-like, from junk pile to junk pile toward the exit.

On the way, they spot Foxtrot carrying a struggling Fixit toward the stasis pod controls. Jetstorm and Russell want nothing more than to help their teammates, but they know they are no match for Decepticons on their own.

Once they are safely outside the scrapyard, the pair hunker down in the woods.

"This isn't right, Jetstorm," Russell pleads. "I have to go back and rescue my dad!"

"I understand, Russell Clay," Jetstorm responds. "But we need help. We need to find Master Drift! Er, and the other bots."

Jetstorm attempts to contact Bumblebee on his wrist communicator, but he only hears static.

Without a message or a map, Russell climbs onto Jetstorm's back once again and the two of them head off in the same direction as their friends, hoping to intercept them in transit.

Back inside the scrapyard, Stilts over-turns an old shark-diving cage to form a makeshift prison for Denny and Slipstream.

"This should keep you out of my gears for now," the Decepticon remarks.

Foxtrot turns to Fixit and points a sharp claw at the Mini-Con. "Release the Ronin," he commands.

Fixit refuses to unlock Forager's stasis pod. "No pay...ray...way!"

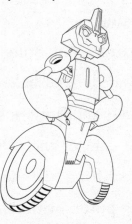

Furious, Foxtrot pulls out a blaster and aims it at the captives.

"I'm feeling a little rusty and could use the target practice!" he sneers.

The twitching Mini-Con reluctantly complies, too nervous to protest again. After a few keystrokes, Forager's cell slips open with a hiss and a pop.

"Ah, whatta nap!" Forager says, stretching and yawning. "I knew I could count on you fellas to spring me."

Forager, Foxtrot, and Stilts exchange an overly complicated handshake with lots of quick movements and jerky jabs.

"Ronin take care of their own, Forager," Foxtrot says, stuffing the no-longer-useful Fixit into the prison with Slipstream and Denny.

"It's funny you guys should mention that,"

Forager replies, popping a lockpick out of his finger and picking absentmindedly at his shiny metal teeth. "Right before I got pinched and stuffed in that cooler, I saw an old buddy palling around with these Autobots. Remember Deadlock? He was that samurai-bot, real into honor and stuff."

Foxtrot and Stilts both look stunned.

"I thought that bot got blasted on the moon of Athena," Foxtrot says.

"Yeah, no one ever saw him after that," Stilts adds, thinking back to that fateful mission. "We figured he was spare parts for sure."

"Well, if he was spare parts, someone sure put him back together well—and slapped an Autobot logo on him as a finishing touch," Forager replies.

The Ronins' trip down memory lane is short-lived, however, as Foxtrot's keen audio receptors pick up the sounds of Bumble-bee, Strongarm, Sideswipe, and Grimlock attempting to sneak back into the scrapyard.

"The Autobots have returned, brothers," Foxtrot informs his fellow mercenaries. His face twists into garish grin. "Shall we escape or take this place over as our new base on Earth?" Stilts and Forager let out wicked cackles.

"As if that was even a question!" Stilts exclaims. "This'll make the perfect hideaway while we plunder and pillage as we please!"

"Sounds peachy, Foxtrot, but it's still three versus four, and I don't like them odds,"

Forager reminds him. "I ain't goin' back in that freezer."

"Don't worry, I think I have an old holo-cloak in my records that'll make this fight a lot more interesting...." Foxtrot replies with a sly smile.

The Decepticon punches a few codes into the display screen on his tail and two small discs pop out. He sticks one to his chest and pockets the other. "I'll save this hologram disc as a surprise."

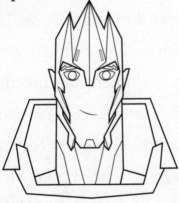

With a press of a button, Foxtrot dons a perfect hologram of Drift or—as they knew him—Deadlock!

"How do I look?" he asks.

"Like a sight for sore optics," Forager replies.

Across the scrapyard, Bumblebee and the others walk nervously toward the diner with their blasters drawn.

As they turn a corner, they see Drift standing with their back to them.

Bumblebee whisper-shouts to their cryptic colleague, but Drift doesn't move or respond.

The Autobot leader walks closer...and closer...reaching out to put his hand on

Drift's shoulder when—*WHOOSH!*—it goes straight through!

"It's a hologram!" Bumblebee shouts to the others—a moment too late.

A second, solid "Drift" leaps out from behind a stack of cars and pins Grimlock to the ground.

"This is an ambush!" the pretend-Drift yells.

Before the big Dinobot can pummel his opponent, he is shocked with an electrical charge.

ZZZARK!

Sideswipe and Strongarm hurry to help their fallen friend, but Stilts and Forager appear and grab them by the wrists.

With a quick spin, the Ronin throw the

two young cadets into each other, knocking them both out!

WHAM!

As pretend-Drift and his allies tie up Bumblebee's teammates, the Autobot leader dashes behind a scrap pile and calls for help.

"Mayday, mayday!" he yells into his communicator's open channel. "Drift and his Decepticons have attacked the scrapyard. If anyone is left, send help!"

"Sorry, little guy," the disguised Foxtrot says, leaning over Bumblebee's hiding spot with Forager and Stilts behind him. "Those nice big wings of Stilts's block signal transmissions. You just spent your last moments of freedom sending out static."

The villains laugh and quickly pile on

Bumblebee, overpowering the struggling hero. Soon, Team Bee is dragged to the stasis pods. As quickly as they were captured, the Autobots are locked away and the Ronin are left in charge of the scrapyard!

Chapter 7

Out in the woods, Jetstorm and Russell continue trudging along in hopes of running into other Autobots. As they near the quarry, Jetstorm picks up on a fragmented communication:

"Mayday, mayday…Drift…attacked…scrap-yard…help!"

"Hey, that's Bumblebee's voice!" Russell says. "But that means Strongarm must have been right—Drift really is a traitor!"

Just as Russell puts Jetstorm's worst fears into words, the two of them look up to see Drift speeding toward them from across the quarry!

"Run!" Russell shouts at Jetstorm.

Jetstorm reluctantly complies, and the young boy hangs on tight as the Mini-Con sprints through the branches.

The roar of Drift's motor gains on them.

VROOOM!

Jetstorm bounces off trees left and right, cutting into a denser part of the forest. Together with Russell, he hides under a big, overturned tree trunk.

Suddenly, a large shadow passes overhead and lands in front of them.

It's Drift!

Russell and Jetstorm scream.

"Why do you flee from your master?" Drift booms, making Jetstorm shrink down on himself.

The Mini-Con may be easily intimidated, but Russell is not. The human climbs off Jetstorm's back and confronts Drift.

"Because you betrayed us!" Russell shouts.

He beats his fists on the cold metal exterior of Drift's shin. "You and your *real* team kidnapped my dad!"

Drift is instantly taken aback. "My 'real team'?" he asks.

"The Decepticons!" Russell yells. "The tall

one with wings and a beak and the mean-looking orange one with the big tail."

Drift's normally calm exterior breaks. He bends down and puts one massive hand around Russell's back to comfort him.

"Russell Clay, I did not attack the others, but I think I know who did," Drift says to the distraught young boy. "You must believe me if we are to rescue them."

Russell looks up into Drift's face, unsure

of what to do, but Jetstorm slowly walks over and kneels in front of Drift.

"I trust you, master," Jetstorm says, eyes averted.

Drift looks at him for a moment.

"Stand, student," he says. "I have not earned your trust. It is time that I come clean about my past. I had hoped to put it behind me, but I see now that my silence has put others at risk."

Drift shifts back into his sleek vehicle mode and opens the door for Russell to get in. Jetstorm takes his place on Drift's side.

Driving back to the scrapyard, Drift explains how he came to know the Ronin.

"Many cycles ago, Cybertron was a very different place," he begins. "When the

Decepticon movement first began, it wasn't clear how evil they were. They spoke about equality and political reform on Cybertron. It was easy to get swept up in all the talk, especially if you started life as a homeless bot stealing Energon just to survive. The skills I learned on the streets drew the attention of Megatron, the leader of the Decepticon movement."

Russell's jaw drops at the mention of Megatron. He's been around the bots long enough to know that Megatron means serious trouble.

"Megatron brought me in, gave me a purpose—and a new name: Deadlock." Drift continues. "I worked alongside the Decepticons for many cycles, watching the movement

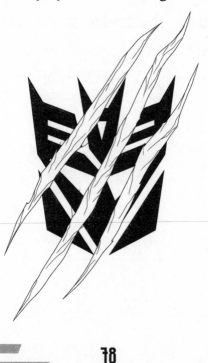

grow increasingly destructive and distanced from its original goals. I did many things I am ashamed of, and for which I can never atone. When I was nearly destroyed in battle, a group of peaceful bots called the Circle of Light repaired me and allowed me to live among them, trading unending conflict for honor and self-control."

Drift sighs, sifting back through painful memories.

"Eventually the war reached even the Circle of Light, and my peace was shattered. For countless cycles after that, I wandered aimlessly, a samurai without a master or a cause. Which is exactly what the Ronin were looking for."

Drift rolls to a halt in the trees surrounding the scrapyard.

"What you must understand about the Ronin is that they answer to no one. Like me, they were Decepticons who grew disenchanted with Megatron's goals. There were many of them, and no single leader. They accepted me without questioning my past deeds. It was…comforting. But in time, I discovered that what they did, they did without honor."

"What did they do?" Russell asks nervously.

"They are bounty hunters, but they recognize no code of virtue. During my final job with them, a group of us followed a bounty to the moon of Athena, a distant planet with a large native population. The target retreated to a sealed bunker deep under the moon's surface. Rather than retreat, one of the Ronin, Foxtrot, suggested blowing the moon apart from space. The explosion would have been devastating to the inhabitants of the planet below."

Russell gasps.

"So what *did* you do?"

"The only thing I could," Drift replies. "When our ship neared bombing range, I set off a small explosion that scared everyone else into the ship's life pods. After they were clear, I triggered the rest of the explosives and then escaped myself. Our ship detonated in orbit. The Ronin were stranded in space until other members of the guild could rescue them, but I fled…determined to follow my path alone, and *with* honor."

His tale done, Drift shifts back into robot mode, letting Russell out first.

Jetstorm again kneels before his master.

"I trust you, master," Jetstorm says.

Drift bows to him.

"I trust you, too, student," Drift responds. "And you, Russell Clay of Earth. Now I ask that you maintain that trust. It will not be easy to defeat the Ronin that have captured your—our—friends. We will need to deceive them."

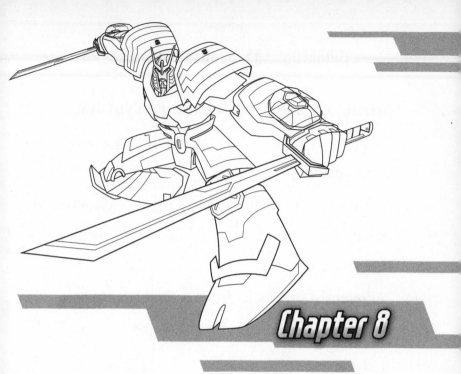

Chapter 8

Drift, Jetstorm, and Russell approach the entrance of the scrapyard. The bright afternoon sun has set, giving the normally welcoming front gate a sinister vibe. A bot that appears to be Grimlock immediately greets them.

"Hello, big bot, small bot, and soft bot,"

pretend-Grimlock says in his dumbest voice. "Me am your Dinobot friend! It am safe to come inside."

"I do not think so, *Stilts*," Drift says, a serious look set on his face. "That is you under there, is it not?"

Pretend-Grimlock frowns and drops his holographic disguise.

"I thought Forager had brain rust when he told us he saw you, Deadlock," Stilts replies. "But it must be *you* with a malfunction if you've allied yourself with these pathetic Autobots."

Without warning, Drift snatches an unsuspecting Russell in one hand and pins Jetstorm to the ground with the other.

"You mean these two?" Drift asks. "I was just tracking down the strays. The Decepticons have a sizable standing bounty for these bots, and I mean to collect."

"Is that so?" Stilts asks, not quite believing Drift's story. "Forager said you seemed pretty chummy with them when he got locked up."

"Do you know of an easier way to capture this many bots solo?" Drift responds without missing a beat. "I was about to start picking them off when Forager blew my cover. Now let me in and we'll discuss how we are going to split the payday."

Stilts still looks unconvinced.

"A nanocycle ago I thought you were nothing but debris drifting through space in a galaxy far, far away," Stilts says. "You're going to have to talk to Foxtrot before I trust anything that comes out of your speech module."

"Oh, is Foxtrot your leader now?" Drift challenges.

"The Ronin have no leader," Stilts says through an angrily clenched beak. "We take care of our own."

The tall Decepticon reluctantly lets Drift in with his struggling prisoners.

When they pass the makeshift holding cell, Drift roughly tosses Russell and Jetstorm inside. Russell just catches the slightest hint of a wink as the former bounty hunter leaves them locked up.

Inside the command center, Foxtrot and Forager are flipping through the prison transport records, taking note of which other members of the Ronin were on board when the ship crashed on Earth. Foxtrot isn't happy to see Drift.

"Shouldn't you be in stasis, traitor?" Foxtrot hisses, flexing his claws.

"Whoa, whoa, wait-a-minute, tough guy," Forager interrupts, putting himself between Foxtrot and Drift. "I'm sure our old pal Deadlock—or should I say *Drift*—has a solid explanation for why he's here and how he's still in one piece."

"There is not much to say," Drift states in his typically stoic fashion. "Our ship went down. I thought *you* blew up. You thought *I* blew up. I work alone now. End of explanation."

"You work alone *until now,* right, old buddy?" Forager says, chuckling.

He wraps a thick arm around Drift's shoulders. "This is fate! We're getting the gang back together. With all them stasis pods and fancy equipment, we can sell the Autobots to the Decepticons and the Decepticons to the Autobots. We'll be rich!"

The cunning crook cackles at his own idea.

"We'll be richer if we don't split the bounties with this backstabber," Foxtrot growls.

"And how long will you waste learning about this equipment and this planet?" Drift asks. "These foolish bots taught me everything."

"Did they teach you how to use the trash

compactor?" Stilts asks. "We were just brainstorming fun ways to deactivate the Mini-Cons. No bounty on those runts."

Drift's face remains calm and unreadable.

"No, but I do know the locations of all the Energon caches they've discovered," Drift says.

The Ronins' optics go wide.

"And we'll need more Energon to power the locators and track down the rest of the bounties," Drift adds. "I've been itching for some action after holding back around these law-bots. Anybot who wants to join me is welcome to follow."

Stilts and Forager look at each other and grin. These rough-and-tumble Decepticons are always up for causing a mess. Foxtrot doesn't hide his distrust of Drift, but he reluctantly joins along.

On the way out of the scrapyard, Forager stops to taunt the prisoners.

"Enjoy the scenery while it lasts, you byte-sized bots," Forager says, rattling the makeshift cage containing Denny, Russell, and the Mini-Cons. "When we come back, we're gonna have fun recycling you."

Drift stands idly by while the Ronin harass his former charges.

When Forager grows tired of the game, they all shift into their vehicle forms and roll out.

Forager turns into a Cybertronian dirt buggy, Foxtrot becomes a sleek alien sports car, and Stilts takes flight as an otherworldly jet plane.

Drift—or, rather, Deadlock—leads the way in his Earth car mode.

Once they are alone, Russell helps his dad

to his feet and turns to Jetstorm with a nervous look on his face.

"So this is still all just an act, right? Drift hasn't betrayed us for real?" Russell asks.

"We will soon find out," the Mini-Con replies.

Chapter 9

"Where are we headed, Deadlock?" Stilts asks, soaring through the air above the other three bots. "Maybe we can try out the old bomb-from-above move again—get it right this time!"

"No need," Drift replies. "The last Decepticon those do-gooders captured hid his stash in an auto factory that should be deserted at this time of night. The native population does not understand Energon, so there was no risk of them stealing it for themselves."

Foxtrot banks a hard turn to the right, fender-checking Drift and nearly pushing him off the road.

"A deserted factory?" Foxtrot growls angrily. "I thought you were taking us someplace we could cut loose and have some fun. If

I wanted to just have a peaceful picnic, I'd have stayed in the woods."

Drift revs his motor and pulls ahead, kicking up dirt and rocks that bounce off Foxtrot's windshield.

"There is no sense in exposing our existence to the humans until we are at full strength," Drift replies curtly.

He grinds to a halt in front of an imposingly large factory, set off from main roads and the general populace of Crown City. The sun is down and all the factory workers are home for the night.

The Ronin switch back into their bot modes, ready to rampage and nab some Energon.

"We'll scale the exterior and enter through the skylight," Drift says."

"No can do, old pal. This bot doesn't climb," Forager says, pointing to himself. "I ain't no good unless I got both paws planted firmly on the ground. Let me take care of this."

The crafty crook pops a lockpick out of his claw to open the large delivery bay doors. Before he can finish tinkering with the lock, Foxtrot steps forward, pulls out his blaster, and shoots a hole through the door.

BLAM!

"Oops," he says sarcastically. "Trigger digit slipped."

"Get a load of this bot, will ya?" Forager

says, slapping Foxtrot on the back. "That's why they call him the Trigger-Happy Terror!"

"That's not what *I* call him," Stilts replies with a smirk.

Foxtrot flashes his teeth at his comrade. "Quit grinding my gears," he snarls.

"Ah, shove it down your intake valve," Stilts retorts.

The bots pile inside, towering above the human-sized proportions.

Stilts's cranium grazes the factory ceiling.

"You know, maybe I better wait outside," he says. "I'm not a big fan of tight spaces."

Foxtrot gives the bot a shove to keep moving and stop complaining.

Drift leads the Ronin to a decommissioned part of the factory, blocked off with yellow caution tape. They smash through equipment and knock over auto parts as they walk along.

"I see you have mastered the art of stealth in my absence," Drift observes dryly.

He directs them toward a hulking tarp-covered shape and pulls the cover off.

The Decepticons have discovered a gargantuan, glowing stack of Energon cubes—ripe for the taking!

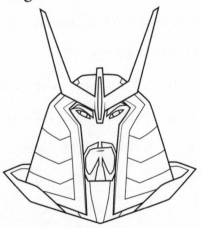

"Well, hello, beautiful!" Forager squeaks.

They each grab as many cubes as they can carry and turn to leave the way they came in.

As they near the exit, Drift is the first to spot a human security guard at the far end of a long hallway. The man is inspecting the smoldering remains of auto parts the Decepticons trashed on their way in.

"This is Officer Wong," the man whispers into a walkie-talkie. "I need to report a serious break-in and a *lot* of damage."

Foxtrot's audio receptors perk up. He turns toward the sound and spies the human.

"Perfect," Foxtrot says, whipping out his blaster. "Some target practice for ol' Trigger-Happy!"

The Decepticon takes aim, but Drift blocks his shot.

"You lack finesse, Foxtrot," Drift says. "*I* will handle this!"

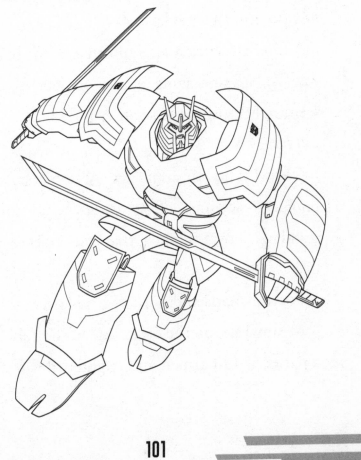

In a flash, Drift unsheathes his sword and spins gracefully through the air. With a blur of movement, his blade slices and dices the ceiling above them. Then he lands without even making a sound.

A moment later, a large portion of the hallway collapses, leaving a pile of debris that seemingly crushes the security guard.

THUD!

"Wow! This samurai has got some style," Forager exclaims. "These fleshbags don't stand a chance against that can opener of his!"

Foxtrot snarls and holsters his blaster.

Meanwhile, on the other side of the rubble, a perfectly unharmed and frightened Officer

Wong hightails it to his police cruiser and speeds away.

With their stashed Energon in tow, the bots hustle out the exit and shift into vehicle mode. Satisfied that their heist is complete, they blaze a trail back to the scrapyard.

Upon their return, the Decepticons dump

their loot near the captives. Their fluids are pumping from the caper, and they finally begin to let down their guard around Drift.

Reminiscing about their old days running the space ways together, Forager reenacts a particularly crazed fight. He waves his arms and fires his blaster all around.

"Then I tried to grease that gearhead's wheels, but he threatened to blow my gasket!" Forager says, finishing his story.

The crook laughs so hard he falls backward. His exhaust pipe starts to sputter and a noxious gas fills the air.

"Filth!" gasps Stilts, covering his beak. "That went right in my vents!"

Forager laughs even harder, and even Foxtrot manages to break a smile.

"Ah yes," says Drift, standing and drawing several *shuriken* from his waist. "I seem to remember bailing your bumper out using... these!"

He slings the throwing stars across the scrapyard, whizzing them through the bars of the jail.

The sharp, spinning blades barely avoid hitting Denny, Russell, and the Mini-Cons, all of whom duck and recoil in fear.

The Ronin laugh uproariously and continue telling old battle tales as they wander off down another corridor.

Once the Decepticons are out of sight, Russell checks out something tied to one of the *shuriken*.

It is a note that reads: *Go now. Release the others.*

Russell shows the note to his fellow captives, a slow smile dawning on each of their faces.

Drift is not a traitor after all!

Slipstream checks the bars near where the *shuriken* entered and realizes that his master had discreetly sliced through the cage door, opening a space large enough for everyone to climb out!

Quickly and quietly, the five escapees slink toward the command center.

Upon reaching the control console, Fixit rapidly types away, and the stasis pods containing Bumblebee, Strongarm, Sideswipe, and Grimlock open up.

WHOOSH!

Bumblebee pops up and shakes the stasis freeze from his optics.

"Come on, team," he says, rallying the bots. "It's time to catch that Drift!"

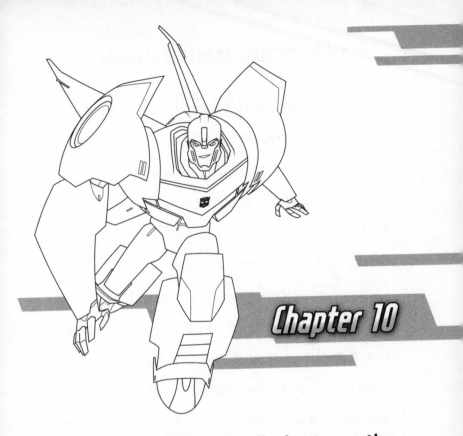

Chapter 10

"Bumblebee, NO!" Russell shouts as the
Autobot leader shifts into vehicle mode. "It's
not what you think! Drift isn't a bad guy!"

"He could have fooled me," Bumblebee responds. "He led us straight into an
ambush."

"That wasn't Drift," Russell explains. "One of the Decepticons can make holograms. Drift was a part of their gang a long time ago, but he quit when they were going to hurt a bunch of people. Jetstorm and I helped Drift infiltrate them to rescue you!"

Bumblebee considers this new information.

"It looks like I might owe Drift an apology if we make it out of this," Bumblebee says. "But right now we need to act before their scanners notice we're out of stasis. Let's go help our teammate, Autobots!"

Team Bee tears through the scrapyard and quickly come face-to-face with the Ronin outside the diner. Without pause, they all leap into battle!

Grimlock barrels his massive bulk at Stilts,

but the nimble bot immediately switches into his plane mode and flies out of reach. He fires at the Dinobot from up high. *CHOOM!*

Strongarm discharges her blaster at Forager, who scurries under a pile of old cars and tunnels out of reach.

"You ain't putting me back in that cell, law-bot!" Forager screams.

Sideswipe sets his sights on Foxtrot, the most deceptive of the Ronin.

The young Autobot flips through the air toward his target—only to smash right through a hologram instead! While Sideswipe regains his bearings, the real Foxtrot appears and delivers a painful blow.

"Flashy but not too bright," the Decepticon says.

As the rest of the team struggles against the Decepticons, Bumblebee dashes straight toward Drift. The samurai instinctively draws his sword.

"This is not as it appears, Bumblebee!" Drift shouts over the din of crashing metal. "I am not a traitor."

Bumblebee grinds to a halt right in front of the samurai-bot.

"I know, and I'm sorry for not trusting you earlier. Your past is behind you. But right now, we have a tough fight ahead of us, and we need to work together."

Bumblebee and Drift exchange curt nods. As Bee joins Sideswipe's fight against Fox-trot, Drift catches up with Grimlock.

The frustrated Dinobot is hurling cars up in the air at Stilts, with little success.

"Grimlock, catch!" Drift yells to the Dinobot, tossing him a small object.

Grimlock looks at the device in his hand.

"This tiny thing?" he exclaims. "I was having better luck with the cars."

"Trust me," Drift says.

The Dinobot winds his arm back and throws the device at the flying Ronin.

"One lob-ball special, coming up!" he announces.

Upon impact, the capsule becomes an expanding net like the one Stilts used to capture Slipstream and Denny.

The net tangles the Decepticon's wings and brings him down in a crash landing.

SMASH!

"Let me out of here! I hate tight spaces!" Stilts cries, twisting and turning on the ground.

"Better get used to it," Grim tells him. "Those stasis pods aren't exactly roomy!"

With Stilts dispatched, Drift and Grimlock sprint over to find Strongarm struggling with Forager, who has tunneled deep into a heap of junked cars. Every time Strongarm gets close, Forager fires his blaster left and right, covering the area.

Drift scans the area and sees the hydraulic lift machine.

"Strongarm, use that construction vehicle to remove his advantage!" Drift instructs her.

Strongarm, cautious to have confidence in Drift's loyalty, leaps behind the wheel of the large lift.

Pulling one lever, Strongarm swings the machine around and knocks over most of the stacked cars, exposing Forager's hiding spot. Then Strongarm flips on the powerful magnetic field, which catches Forager and drags the kicking and screaming Ronin high off the ground.

CLANG!

"Lemme go! Lemme go!" Forager yips. "I don't like heights!"

"Hang in there," Strongarm says smugly.

She joins Drift and Grimlock, and the trio race toward the fight against Foxtrot.

When they turn the corner, they find that Bumblebee and Sideswipe are not fighting the single remaining Ronin—they're tussling with over fifty Foxtrots!

"I know most of them are holograms, but the real Ronin keeps attacking us while we're distracted!" Sideswipe tells Drift, bringing him up to speed.

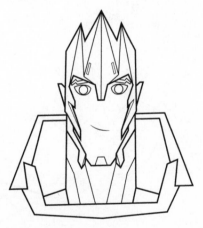

Drift thinks for a moment.

"Everybot stay calm and close your optics," Drift says.

"I thought you were on our side! Are you trying to get us blasted?" Strongarm asks.

"Do what Drift says, cadet!" Bumblebee orders. "Trust your instincts!"

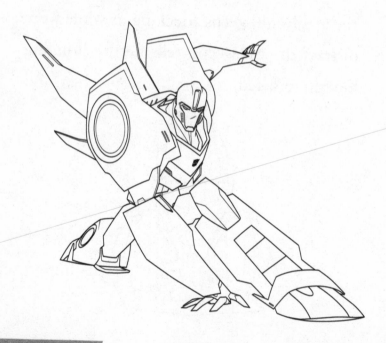

The five Autobots stand totally silent, shoulder-to-shoulder and back-to-back. After a nanocycle of concentration, one noise breaks through the din of holographic humming: the clinking of Foxtrot unlatching his sidearm!

"There!" the bots all shout in unison.

Bumblebee, Strongarm, and Sideswipe point their plasma cannons and fire. The real Foxtrot takes three simultaneous hits and staggers back.

Projection discs crunch underfoot as Grimlock tramples across the scrapyard, extinguishing holograms left and right.

Foxtrot tries to make a break for it, but Drift gets a running start and tackles him to the ground.

"Ronin take care of their own," Drift says. "And you've been outfoxed."

He delivers a wallop of a punch right to Foxtrot's snout, laying him out flat!

POW!

Grimlock brings one massive foot down on the Ronin's tail, preventing him from crawling away.

"You may have defeated the Ronin, Deadlock," Foxtrot whispers, struggling under the Dinobot's weight. "But you can never change who you really are."

"There is no Deadlock, only Drift now," the reformed Autobot says.

"And *Drift* was never wicked like you to begin with," Bumblebee adds.

The Autobot leader turns toward Drift and reaches out his hand. "I apologize, Drift. I should have trusted you."

"Your apology is not necessary, Bumblebee," Drift replies, shaking his hand. "I did not trust you all with my past, and it became a danger to us. It is not in my nature to be so…open…but I vow to do better."

The Autobots help carry the rest of the bad

bots back to the stasis pods, where Russell, Denny, and the Mini-Cons are waiting.

Drift bows before Slipstream and Jetstorm.

"I humbly seek your forgiveness, students," he says.

Jetstorm and Slipstream look at each other, unsure of how to respond. They bow in return.

"We humbly grant it, master," the Mini-Cons reply in unison.

"Even though I am your master, I am still learning as well," Drift says quietly. "Today I have learned the virtue of trust, and that running from your past will only leave you to confront it alone and unprepared."

Grimlock surprises Drift with a big Dino-bot embrace.

"Welcome back!" he cheers.

"It is also not in my nature...to be so... close," grunts Drift.

The Autobots laugh and congratulate one another on another mission accomplished.

"I guess we do make a great team after all," Bumblebee says to Drift.

"And *you* make a great leader, Bumblebee," Drift replies. He bows to the yellow Autobot commander.

Bumblebee returns the gesture.

Drift helps his teammates load Foxtrot, Forager, and Stilts into stasis. As the pods slide shut, locking away the Ronin criminals, Drift can feel his past as Deadlock disappear with them.

He is no longer a Decepticon, a masterless samurai, or a Ronin fighting only for himself. He is an Autobot, fighting for Earth…and for his new friends!

Bumblebee
Versus
Scuzzard

Turn the page
for a sneak peek!

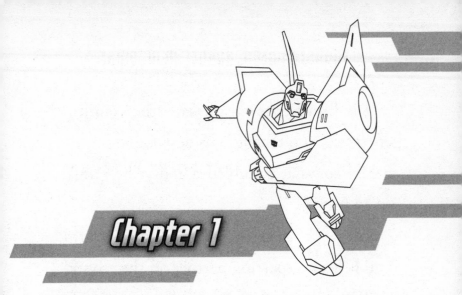

Chapter 1

"Stop in your tracks, Decepticon!" shouts
Bumblebee. "You're under arrest!"

The Autobot leader blasts his plasma
cannon. The rapidly moving target leaps
from side to side then somersaults over the
Cybertronian lieutenant, landing behind
him. The agile adversary shoves Bumblebee
to the ground.

"Is that the best you got, law-bot?" taunts a
familiar voice.

It is Bumblebee's teammate: the youthful, energetic, and rebellious Sideswipe.

He scowls at Bumblebee and yells, "You're scrap metal!"

Sideswipe then smiles, extends his arm, and helps his sparring partner off the ground.

"Pretty impressive," Bumblebee says. "You've got some nice moves, but the tough-bot attitude might be a bit over the top, don't you think?"

The young Autobot laughs. "You got to be a tough-bot if you want to intimidate those Decepticons, Bee."

"Thanks for the advice," Bumblebee replies. "Who's next?"

The Autobot leader scans the scrapyard

that currently serves as their headquarters and training area.

Located on the outskirts of Crown City on planet Earth, the scrapyard belongs to a pair of humans: Denny Clay and his son, Russell. The Clays have befriended Bumblebee and his robot team and sometimes help them on their mission to track down and capture a number of Decepticon fugitives from the planet Cybertron.

"It is my turn, sir," calls out Strongarm. The young cadet dutifully strides over to the center of the training area.

Back on Cybertron, Strongarm was a member of the police force serving under Lieutenant Bumblebee. Now she helps serve and protect anyone or anything that may come to harm at the hands of the Autobots' evil enemies on Earth.

"Let's see if your moves are as good as mine," Sideswipe says to her. "Not everyone gets the best of Bee. But *I* did!"

"Show some respect, Sideswipe," replies Strongarm. "You may have advanced 'street smarts' back home, but you're no intellitron. Bumblebee is your commanding officer, and you should treat him as such!"

"You're right," snaps Sideswipe. "So I only have to listen to *him*. Not you!"

"Fine," huffs the police-bot. "Who says I want to waste nanocycles talking to *you* anyway?" Strongarm retorts. "I'd have to use smaller words and talk...very...slowly."

"Enough!" Bumblebee says, exasperated. "We are all on the *same* team, whether we like to admit it or not. The real foes are out there and we need to be prepared. Something terrible is on the horizon, and by the AllSpark, I sure hope we can handle it!"

"Yes, sir," Strongarm says. "Let's continue training."

"Where are Grimlock and Drift?" Sideswipe asks.

Grimlock is a Dinobot and former Decepticon who defected to the Autobots, and Drift is an honorable bounty hunter. They're also part of Bumblebee's ragtag team.

"Drift has a free pass from today's training," Bumblebee replies. "He took the Groundbridge to an area with an allegedly high concentration of Energon. You know how he likes his solo missions."

"Yeah, Drift sure is a real-deal tough-bot," Sideswipe says. "Glad he's on our side."

Bumblebee chuckles. "I asked him to recon and report back," the leader says. "If there is Energon out there, we'll travel to the location and harvest the power source right away."

"Excellent," Strongarm cheers. "Another mission!"

"I totally understand your enthusiasm, Strongarm," Bumblebee replies. "Things have been a little quiet around here."

"Yeah, quiet until the storm hits," Sideswipe says, slamming his fist into his palm. "I'm ready for whatever the Decepticons got!"

"I have a feeling the Decepticons may be

after something as big and as powerful as the AllSpark."

Strongarm gasps. "But, sir, harnessing that kind of power could bring about unimaginable destruction!"

Bumblebee nods grimly.

Sideswipe breaks the uncomfortable silence and tries to lighten the mood. "Speaking of destruction, what's Grimlock up to?"

"He's recharging on top of a pile of old cars," a voice answers.

The Autobots turn to see Russell, their twelve-year-old human friend. "Grimlock found a nice sunny spot, and he's lying in it like a big lizard."

"Hey, Russell," Bumblebee says. "What's up?"

"Shouldn't you be at lob-ball practice?" asks Sideswipe.

Russell chuckles. "Here on Earth, it's called football."

"Oh, right," Sideswipe says, trying to remember the word. "Foot. Ball."

"We're on spring break from school," Russell continues.

"Spring break?" Strongarm asks, puzzled.

"Yeah."

Suddenly, Fixit rolls into the training area from behind a dented billboard.

"Who has a spring break?" Fixit asks. "It's about time! I've been itching to repaint... repeat... repair something."

The multitasking Mini-Con was pilot of the prison transport ship *Alchemor*—the same ship that crashed to Earth and let loose the Decepticon criminals aboard. Now he rounds out the rest of Team Bee as the resident handy-bot.

After the crash, Fixit developed a minor stutter, but he manages to correct his vocabulary with a quick check.

The Mini-Con weaves in and out between the legs of the Autobots, twitching his digits excitedly.

"No one had anything break," Bumblebee says, looking himself over. "As far as I can tell."

Russell laughs. "Spring break is another term for taking a vacation from school."

"What's a vacation?" Strongarm asks.

"It's time off," Sideswipe replies. "Like an extended holiday."

Strongarm's optics open wide with surprise. "Who would want to take time off from school?"

"Not Miss Perfect Attendance, I'm sure," Sideswipe retorts.

"Every single cycle!" Strongarm announces proudly.

"Really? I'm impressed, cadet," Bumblebee says. "That's an excellent record!"

"I know!" Strongarm beams.

Sideswipe rolls his optic sensors.

"Anyway," Russell interrupts. "My friends Hank and Butch are going away with their families for the next week and, well, I'm kind of stuck here, where nothing exciting has happened in *ages*."

The boy kicks a rock and sits on an

overturned shopping cart.

"That's not so bad," Fixit replies. "I'm stumped…stunned…stuck here all the time when all the other bots are out on missions or when they play games together."

"Every team member's duty is very important," Bumblebee explains. "Especially yours, Fixit."

Sideswipe sighs. "All right. There's only so much sappy goodness this bot can take before he gets brain rust."

He walks over and crouches near the Mini-Con.

"So, you *really* wanna play lob-ball with us? You got it!"

With a loud whistle, the red robot wakes up Grimlock.

"Big G!" Sideswipe hollers. "We're playing lob-ball with Fixit. Go long!

"Finally!" Grimlock exclaims as he stretches his limbs. "Something to do that involves some action!"

Fixit rubs his digits together with anticipation and excitement.

"Excellent. What's my position?"

Sideswipe smirks and picks up the Mini-Con.

"Ball," he says.

Then, in one deft movement, he hurls Fixit through the air straight at Grimlock.

"AAAAAAAAAH!" screams the Mini-Con as he becomes a tiny dot against the sky.

Bumblebee sighs and hangs his head.

"When I said we need to focus on working as a team, this is not what I had in mind."